Our **WILD**™
WORLD
SERIES

Lions

NorthWord Press
Minnetonka, Minnesota

DEDICATION
To Dr. Paul Bingham, Dr. Mark Ryan, and the entire staff of the Redstone Veterinary Hospital,
with deepest thanks on behalf of my own little lioness

Photography © 2001: Barbara Gerlach/Visuals Unlimited: front cover; Tom & Pat Leeson: pp. 4, 38-39; Mitsuaki Iwago
/Minden Pictures: pp. 5, 16, 18, 30; Anup Shah: pp. 6, 24-25, 26; Stephen G. Maka: pp. 7, 34; Frans Lanting/Minden Pictures:
pp. 8-9; Rich Kirchner: pp. 11, 15, 22-23, 41; Robert E. Barber/Visuals Unlimited: p. 12; Gavriel Jecan/Art Wolfe, Inc.: p. 20;
Michael H. Francis: p. 27; Craig Packer: pp. 28-29; Gerald & Buff Corsi/Visuals Unlimited: pp. 32-33; Gerry Ellis/Minden
Pictures: p. 37; Robin Brandt: p. 42; Erwin & Peggy Bauer: back cover, pp. 44-45.

All photographs in this book are of African lions unless noted.

Illustrations by John F. McGee
Designed by Russell S. Kuepper
Edited by Barbara K. Harold

NorthWord Press
5900 Green Oak Dr
Minnetonka, MN 55343
1-800-328-3895

Library of Congress Cataloging-in-Publication Data

Winner, Cherie.
    Lions / author, Cherie Winner ; illustrations, John F. McGee.
      p. cm. -- (Our wild world series)
    ISBN 1-55971-787-4 (soft cover) ISBN 1-55971-806-4 (hard cover)
      1. Lions--Juvenile literature. [1. Lions.] I. McGee, John F. ill. II. Title. III. Series.

QL737.C23 W555 2001
599.757--dc21   2001022212

Printed in Singapore

10 9 8 7 6 5 4 3 2 1

Our WILD™ WORLD SERIES

Lions

Cherie Winner
Illustrations by John F. McGee

NORTHWORD PRESS
Minnetonka, Minnesota

THE STORY OF LIONS is filled with danger. It is a story of fierce battles over territory and who will mate. It is a story of hunting for food and survival.

The lion is often called the "King of the Jungle." But lions don't live in jungles. They live on grassy plains, where they hunt antelopes, zebras, and other animals. They also live in areas called open forests, where trees mix with the grassland.

Lions once lived in Africa, Europe, the Middle East, and southern Asia. As humans built towns and farms in these areas, many lions were killed. Others died because they could no longer find enough food. Some moved to places where there weren't so many people.

Today lions live in a much smaller area than they once did. About 21,000 lions still roam in eastern and southern Africa. Only about 200 Asian lions still live in the Gir National Park and Lion Sanctuary in western India.

Lions have keen eyesight
to help them hunt.

Females are very protective of their babies,
and watch over them very carefully.

This resting Asian male lion may not look dangerous, but he becomes extremely fierce when he must protect his territory, or home area.

The lion's scientific name is *Panthera leo*. Lions belong to the Felidae (FEE-lih-dee), or cat, family. They are the second-largest members of the cat family, after tigers. In Africa, adult male lions stand about 48 inches (1.2 meters) high at the shoulder and weigh about 420 pounds (189 kilograms). Females are smaller. They grow to 44 inches (1.1 meters) tall and weigh about 275 pounds (124 kilograms). In India, male lions weigh about 400 pounds (180 kilograms) and females weigh about 250 pounds (113 kilograms).

This female is almost completely camouflaged as she watches for enemies as well as food.

Most lions have golden fur that works like camouflage (KAM-uh-flaj) to blend in with the long grasses. Some lions have dark brown fur, and some are much lighter in color, almost white. A lion's belly and chest are also light, often white.

Whatever the color, lion coats have two layers, a soft layer of thick underfur covered by coarse outer guard hairs. These layers protect lions from harsh sun, chilly winds, and soaking rain. Their lips are black, and their eyes are dark yellow. Many lions have a narrow patch of pale hair just under the eyes.

These young lions have found a good place to rest, high off the ground.

All lions have a long tail with a tuft of black hair at the tip, like a paintbrush. The tail is just long enough to touch the ground when the lion stands up. When a lion runs, it holds the tail up or to one side to help it keep its balance.

Lions are the only cats that have a mane, which is a ring of bushy hair on the head, neck, and shoulders. Maybe it is the mane that makes a lion look like a "king." Only males have a mane. It develops as the young male lion becomes an adult.

The mane can be the same color as the lion's back, or it might be silver, orange, or very dark brown. Strong males usually have a long, dark mane. It is important for a female to mate with a strong male, so their offspring will be strong, too. The bushier, darker mane attracts her to the best choice.

Some African lions have such thick manes that it's hard to see their ears. The manes of Asian lions aren't as bushy, so their ears can easily be seen. In both kinds of lions, the front of each ear is about the same color as the lion's back, or a little lighter. On the back of each ear is a broad stripe or patch of black fur.

The ears are round, and they face forward most of the time. Lions don't often turn their ears to hear better, as many other animals do. They do turn their ears to the back or to the side to warn other lions to stay away. When they turn their ears, the black fur on the back of the ears can be seen.

Lions
FUNFACT:

Young lions sometimes climb trees, but adult lions in the wild seldom do.

Grooming, or cleaning, is important for lions. They regularly clean themselves with their rough tongues. Sometimes they clean each other.

Along both sides of the lion's long snout are several rows of whiskers. These are long, sensitive hairs that help the lion navigate, or find its way, at night. If a lion walks so close to a tree or a boulder that its whiskers touch it, the lion will turn a bit so it doesn't run into the object.

On the face near the whiskers are several rows of small, black spots. They make a pattern that is different for every lion, just as fingerprints are different for every person. Scientists who study animals are called zoologists (zoe-OL-uh-jists). They use these spot patterns to identify individual lions.

The hair on a lion's face is quite short, but the hair of the mane often grows to 20 inches (51 cm) long.

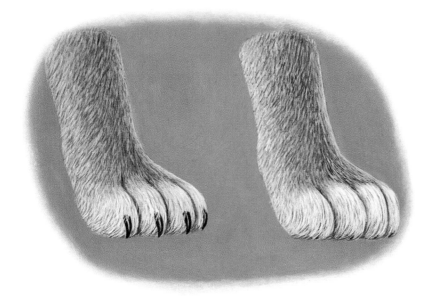

Zoologists also study other parts of the face to learn how old the lion is. If its teeth are yellow and worn down, the lion is probably over 12 years old. The color of the tip of the nose gives clues, too. Young lions' noses are pink and black. As they get older, the black areas get bigger until finally, sometime after they turn five years old, the whole tip of the nose is black.

You can tell by looking at their claws and teeth that lions are carnivores (KAR-nuh-vorz), or meat eaters. They are also predators (PRED-uh-tors), which means they catch and kill the animals they eat, called prey (PRAY).

The long, sharp claws curve downward so the lion can hold on to the prey animal. When a lion is resting, its claws are tucked inside its toes. When it grabs the prey, special muscles make the claws stick out. This kind of claw is called retractile (ree-TRAK-tul). Lions also use their claws to get good traction when they run. They keep their claws sharp by scratching on trees.

A lion has 30 teeth in all. The long, pointed canine (KAY-nine) teeth at the front corners of the mouth are very important. Each lion has two canine teeth in the upper jaw and two in the lower jaw. Lions use their canine teeth to get a good grip on their prey so it can't escape. Their jaws are very strong. Lions usually kill their prey by suffocating it. That means they keep it from breathing. They do this by biting through the throat or by grabbing on to the snout. Either way, the prey cannot breathe and dies quickly.

Farther back in the lion's mouth are four large teeth with jagged edges, called carnassial (kar-NASS-ee-ul) teeth. There are two carnassials on each side of the mouth, one in the upper jaw and one in the lower jaw. When the lion bites down, these teeth work like scissors to cut through the meat. The lion's other teeth are also sharp and help the lion hold on to prey and tear meat.

Lions
FUNFACT:

You can tell if an adult lion has been in the area by the signs it leaves on the ground. Each paw print is about the size of a saucer or small plate. A lion's scat, or dropping, is about the size and shape of a banana.

A lion's canine teeth may be 2 to 2½ inches (5 to 6 cm) long.
It can open its jaw 11 inches (28 cm) wide.

When a herd of cape buffalo notices a group of lions hunting in the area, they fiercely protect themselves and their young.

The kind of meat they eat depends on how healthy the lions are and how many lions are hunting. Lions get about one-fourth of their meat by scavenging (SKAV-en-jing), or eating prey that was killed by other animals. Lions will chase hyenas, cheetahs, or other smaller predators away from their kills and steal the food. This seems like an easy way to eat, but the lions never know when they will find such a meal. They usually rely on their hunting skills to catch their own dinner.

Lions that are old or weak usually hunt small prey such as rabbits, birds, or snakes. Healthy lions hunting alone usually go for larger prey such as zebra and antelope. Lions in groups will even hunt big animals like hippopotamuses or cape buffalo.

Lions find their prey mostly by sight and by sound. Lions can see and hear much better than humans can. Their sense of smell is much less important for their hunting than it is for many other wild animals. When hunting during the day or early evening, lions rely mostly on their keen vision to see prey in the distance. When hunting in the dark, their hearing also becomes important. But even then, they depend on their eyesight. Lions can see so much better at night than the animals they are hunting, that they have a big advantage.

Lions also know where prey are most likely to be. Water holes are favorite hunting spots. There aren't many places to find water on the plains, so a good water hole, which is like a large pond, attracts many animals every day. Lions know that if they wait long enough at a water hole, they will have a chance to catch a big dinner.

Because zebras can run for long distances, a lion's best hunting strategy is to surprise the zebra and catch it quickly.

A lion's top speed is about 40 miles (64 kilometers) per hour, but only for short distances. Many prey animals can easily outrun a lion. Fortunately, lions have other skills that are important for hunters. They can change direction or stop in an instant. They are also very patient and very powerful. Sometimes a lion will stalk, or quietly follow, its prey. They usually don't stalk for a long time. Instead of following their prey over long distances, they hide in long grass until the prey comes close. Then they jump out of their hiding place. Lions can leap about 40 feet (12 meters) in one bound. Within a few strides they catch the startled prey.

Sometimes lions cooperate, or work together, to bring down the prey. Several lions may surround the prey, gradually closing in on it. Or one lion may chase the prey toward other lions hiding in the grass or behind large rocks.

Lions
FUNFACT:

Lions hunting in pairs or groups catch their prey about 1 time in 3 tries. Lions hunting alone need to try about 6 times to get their dinner.

Even while taking a refreshing drink at a water hole, lions are always watching for possible prey nearby. Lions can swim, but they usually avoid it.

When a lion hunts alone and kills a small prey, it usually keeps it to itself. If a lion kills a large prey, or if two or more lions team up during the hunt, other members of the family group, or pride, come to share the feast. Many lions crowd around the meat, each one trying to get as much of it as possible. Females let the young lions, or cubs, eat at the same time, but male lions sometimes keep other members of the pride away until they are full. Cubs may have to wait for their turn.

When they make a big kill, lions gorge themselves, or eat as much as they can. After the big meal, lions might not hunt and eat again for several days. In the meantime, all members of the pride sleep a lot. In fact, lions sleep or rest for about 19 hours of every day. That is why lions have the reputation for being lazy!

The females of a pride often rest together. They prefer to find a
high place where they can see in all directions.

All the female lions in a pride are related. They are sisters, mothers, daughters, aunts, cousins, or nieces to each other. A female lion, or lioness, lives her whole life in the pride she was born into.

Young males always leave their birth pride when they are about three years old. They go looking for another pride to live with, in order to mate and produce offspring.

Some prides have just one adult male and two adult females and their cubs. Other prides have up to 30 members. Most have around 15 members. Areas with more prey have bigger prides.

Within the pride, different jobs are done by different lions. Females do most of the hunting. Males patrol the pride's territory and defend it against other male lions.

Pages 24-25: These two strong males are traveling together, patrolling their territory.

This lioness can warm herself in the sun while she watches over her territory.

A territory is the area where the pride lives and hunts. In places with lots of prey, it may be only 25 square miles (65 square kilometers). In places with less prey, a lion must search farther for food. The territory might be as large as 250 square miles (648 square kilometers). The lions move around within their territory to follow the prey. They go where the prey animals go.

Lions guard their territory by roaring and by scent (SENT) marking. A roar is a deep, loud sound. It is the loudest sound made by any kind of cat. It is even louder than a jackhammer or a sandblasting machine. A lion's roar can be heard up to 5 miles (8 kilometers) away.

Moving across the savanna in search of food, lions move quietly. They really walk on their toes, making good use of the cushioned pads on their paws.

Lions roar mainly at dawn and at sunset. Lions are usually standing when they roar, but they can also roar while sitting or lying down. They don't do it to scare prey. Lions roar to say "We are a family," "This area is ours," and "Other lions, stay away!" If male lions hear another lion roar near their pride, or even if they hear a zoologist's tape recording of a lion roaring, they immediately go to chase it away.

Another way lions claim their territory is by leaving their scent, or odor. Lions do this by urinating on the ground or rubbing against trees and bushes. They do this all throughout their territory, not just around its borders.

Besides hunting and protecting their territory, the main business of the pride is raising young. Usually, all the females in a pride are ready to mate at about the same time. That way all the cubs are born about the same time. They eat, sleep, play, and grow up together.

These females from a pride have become very good at hunting together.

The muscles of this female lion's back legs are very strong for leaping at prey.

When a lioness is ready to mate, she urinates more often. Her urine carries a special scent that tells the males she is ready. She also makes a long, low call that sounds like a rumble.

The first male to reach the female when she is ready is usually the one that gets to mate with her. If two males get there about the same time, they challenge each other. They turn their ears so the backs of them face forward. Their tails twitch and they lean forward and hiss at each other. Sometimes the weaker one gives up without fighting, but sometimes the stronger one must swat him with a heavy paw before he will leave. When one lion decides the other lion is stronger, his ears go flat against his head. He sinks to the ground and slowly crawls away.

The winning male guards his female and keeps her away from all the other males for several days. They don't eat during this time.

About 110 days after mating, the female gives birth. A week or so before this, she finds a sheltered place to use as a den site.

Lions usually don't have an actual den, like a cave or a tunnel into the ground. Instead they just need an area where the cubs are safe from storms and hidden from predators. It may be a place between boulders or under the overhanging edge of a dry riverbed.

A pride may use the same den site many times over the years, but they also stay alert for new sites that other animals don't know about yet.

Sometimes other animals discover the den site. Then the mother lion picks up each cub by the scruff of its neck and moves them all to a new den site.

If the new den site is not far, one or more of the cubs may walk on their own. Others may need help from their mother.

This den site is well protected from storms and well camouflaged from predators.

A mother lion may have as many as six cubs, but she usually has two or three. Each cub weighs just 2 to 4 pounds (0.9 to 1.8 kilograms). They are about the size of a soda-pop can, with stubby little legs. Their eyes stay closed until they are about 11 days old, and their first set of teeth comes in three to four weeks after birth.

Newborn cubs don't move much except to drink their mother's milk. The mother lion nurses her cubs for about eight hours every day. She keeps them warm by curling her body around them. She keeps them clean by licking up their urine and droppings. This keeps the den site from smelling and attracting hyenas or other predators that might kill the cubs.

During their first few weeks of life, the mother lion stays with her cubs most of the time. She only leaves when she needs to find food or water for herself. All the mother lions go hunting together. They are safer in a group. While the females hunt, they leave their cubs hidden in the den sites. The cubs stay very quiet.

Lions
FUNFACT:

Both males and females roar, but males do it more often.

The cubs can walk well by the time they are about five weeks old. Then their mother leads them away from their den site to join the rest of the pride. They meet the adults and other cubs, which become their playmates.

Every mother lion lets any cub in the group nurse from her. When she's awake, a mother may push away a cub that is not her own. But as soon as she dozes off, other cubs can snuggle up next to her and nurse from her.

Even with many adults around to protect them, more than half of the cubs die before they are one year old. Some are eaten by animals such as leopards. Some die of disease. If their mothers are having trouble finding food, they don't make enough milk, and the cubs starve.

As the survivors grow, their looks change, as well as what they eat, and what they are able to do for themselves.

When this mother takes her cub away from the den site,
she teaches it new things about the habitat.

Cubs don't learn everything from their mother. They also learn many things from playing with each other.

At first, cubs have fuzzy brown or orange spots on their fluffy coats, which help to camouflage the cubs at the den site. Over time, the spots fade. Their coats become smooth and shiny. Young males grow long tufts of hair on their neck and shoulders. Eventually they develop a bushy mane like their fathers, but the mane won't be full size until the lions are about five years old.

At first, cubs get all their nourishment from their mother's milk. During this time, their mother brings dead prey near the cubs. She eats it in front of them so they can learn what adult lions eat. When they are about six weeks old, they start eating meat, too. Their baby teeth have come in so they are able to tear small pieces of meat. They continue to nurse until they are eight to ten months old, but they get more and more of their nourishment from meat.

When they are about six months old, their adult teeth start to come in. The cubs also start learning how to hunt. They follow along to watch how the females hunt.

Sometimes their mother brings them prey that she has injured, and lets them practice killing it. Often the cubs just want to play with the prey. At first, they don't know they must kill it in order to eat, but they soon understand what to do.

They learn to stalk silently by trying to sneak up on each other. They learn how to hide, how to wait patiently, and how to surprise their target by jumping out at just the right moment.

Hunting takes a lot of practice. Young lions don't kill prey on their own until they are at least 15 months old, and it takes many more weeks of practice before they are really good at it. Until then, they depend on their mother and the other adult females in the pride for their food.

One thing that makes hunting so hard to learn is that lions go after large animals that are big enough to fight back. They can bite, or strike out with their sharp hooves, or slash their pointed horns across a lion's tender belly. In order to be a good hunter, a lion must learn how to protect itself as well as how to find and kill the prey.

Lions
FUNFACT:

Until about 10,000 years ago, lions could be found from Alaska and Yukon in North America to as far south as Peru in South America. They died out, or became extinct, because many of their prey animals became extinct.

Before they are ready to go hunting with the rest of the pride, cubs get practice by pretending to stalk and pounce on each other.

Finally, when they are two years old, the young lions can hunt for themselves. Young females stay with the pride. In two more years, they also will be ready to mate and raise a family.

Their brothers, however, are not allowed to stay with the pride. They are chased away by their mother. The young males from the pride usually stay together their whole life. They make up a group called a coalition (koe-uh-LIH-shun). Sometimes one male from another pride joins them. Their coalition lives and hunts together, and searches for a pride to join.

Like females in a pride, most males in a coalition are related.
A coalition may have only 2 members or as many as 9 members.

Male lions that are already with a pride don't want other males around, so when a new coalition comes along, they fight. The males bite and claw each other. Some of them even die.

If the pride lions win, life goes on as usual and the strangers go away. If the pride lions lose, they go off to live on their own. They will not live with a pride again. Soon, within a few months or a few years, they die.

The winning strangers kill all the cubs in the pride. Then, with those cubs out of the way, they mate with the females to produce cubs of their own. In some areas, more cubs die from being killed by male lions than from any other cause.

Lions
FUNFACT:

A male can eat 95 pounds (43 kilograms) of meat in one day. A female can eat 55 pounds (25 kilograms).

Life is very dangerous for lions, especially for males and for cubs. Males that don't live with a pride constantly look for a pride to take over. Those that do live with a pride must always guard against coalitions trying to take their place. Male lions in eastern Africa live for about 12 years. In India, they live to be about 16 years old.

No matter which group of males wins the battles over the prides, lionesses stay in their birth pride. Females in eastern Africa and India live to be 18 years or older. They mate and raise cubs until they are 15 years old. They provide food for their pride and teach their offspring about hunting.

The male lion, with his magnificent mane and fearsome roar, may be "king." But the female, with her keen hunting and mothering skills, is the true center of the lion pride.

This healthy male and female are enjoying a
good rest in their lush habitat.

Internet Sites

You can find out more interesting information about lions and lots of other wildlife by visiting these internet sites.

http://endangered.fws.gov/kids/index.html	U.S. Fish and Wildlife Service
www.discovery.com	Discovery Channel Online
www.asiatic-lion.org	Asiatic Lion Information Centre
www.EnchantedLearning.com	Enchanted Learning
www.kidsplanet.org	Defenders of Wildlife
www.lionresearch.org	The Lion Research Center
www.nationalgeographic.com/kids	National Geographic Society
www.nwf.org/kids	National Wildlife Federation
www.tnc.org	The Nature Conservancy
www.wcs.org	Wildlife Conservation Society
www.worldwildlife.org/fun/kids.cfm	World Wildlife Fund

Index

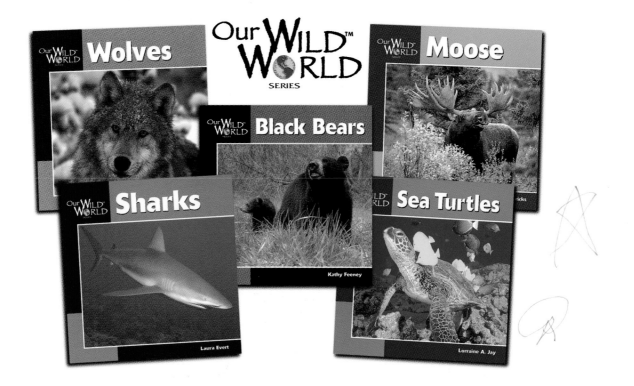

Paperback titles available in the Our Wild World Series:

BISON
ISBN 1-55971-775-0

LIONS
ISBN 1-55971-787-4

WHALES
ISBN 1-55971-780-7

BLACK BEARS
ISBN 1-55971-742-4

MANATEES
ISBN 1-55971-778-5

WHITETAIL DEER
ISBN 1-55971-743-2

COUGARS
ISBN 1-55971-788-2

MOOSE
ISBN 1-55971-744-0

WOLVES
ISBN 1-55971-748-3

DOLPHINS
ISBN 1-55971-776-9

SEA TURTLES
ISBN 1-55971-746-7

EAGLES
ISBN 1-55971-777-7

SHARKS
ISBN 1-55971-779-3

See your nearest bookseller, or order by phone 1-800-328-3895

NORTHWORD PRESS
Minnetonka, Minnesota